Oliver's Tale

by

Stephen James

Copyright © 2024 Stephen James

ISBN: 978-1-917293-50-1

All rights reserved, including the right to reproduce this book, or portions thereof in any form. No part of this text may be reproduced, transmitted, downloaded, decompiled, reverse engineered, or stored, in any form or introduced into any information storage and retrieval system, in any form or by any means, whether electronic or mechanical without the express written permission of the author.

The views expressed in this work are solely those of the author and do not necessarily reflect the views of the publisher, and the publisher hereby disclaims any responsibility for them.

Hb

All illustrations in this book are by David Dudley

www.totalpencilportraits.co.uk

Also by Stephen James: 'The Mad World of a Village Postman' published 2021

This book is for our Great Mate, Oliver. Such a lovely chap who has taught us so much about living with a Cat.

Oliver

Oliver is a well-mannered black cat with a white nose, vest and socks. The vet believes that he is 2-3 years old and is rather large for his age. In fact, he is rather large for any age.

Oliver adopted a family in Eastbourne that he lived with for just over a year. He was given the name Oliver because he always asked for more. When the people Oliver lived with could no longer look after him, it was obvious that he was going to need a new home. Oliver's owner told friends and work colleagues about the situation, and he was given a new home in Bexhill. Oliver was most unhappy about this turn of events to begin with, but after plenty of attention and reassurance, he soon settled into his new surroundings.

The Two Charlies

Steve and Jayne moved to a bungalow in Bexhill-on-Sea and not long after moving in, they were visited by a small black cat. Although neither of them had any previous experience, or indeed interest in cats, they befriended the little chap. Initial enquiries locally failed to find his previous home, so they began looking after the cat and named him Tinker.

Tinker then suddenly disappeared and after making some enquiries, it turned out that he was known to some of the local residents and apparently, it was quite normal for him to behave in this way. He would spend several weeks at one house and then move on to another. Steve and Jayne had enjoyed the experience of having Tinker around and they missed him.

While Tinker was absent, Jayne was asked by a work colleague if she could give her cat, Oliver, a new home. After several days of thinking that a kitten would suit them better, Steve and Jayne agreed to have a look at Oliver anyway. He seemed to be quite a character and they decided to give him a go.

About a week after Oliver had arrived in Bexhill, Tinker re-appeared. Steve and Jayne tried not to encourage him, but he was obviously not well. A trip to the vet was deemed necessary and his prospects were not looking good. Despite several weeks of persevering with Tinker's health problems and resultant bad habits, a second trip to the vet meant that the end had come for the little chap. If it had not been for him, however, Oliver might not have come to live in Bexhill at all.

The Writing of Oliver's Tale

When Oliver's previous owner resigned from her job, Jayne suggested to Steve that it might be a nice idea to give her soon-to-be ex-colleague a card from Oliver to wish her luck in the future. Steve took the idea of a card a step further and penned a letter from Oliver telling her about his new life in Bexhill. The letter was enjoyed by Oliver's previous owner and her work colleagues. Thus it was suggested that Oliver should continue, just for fun, to let his friends know of his adventures and experiences as he adjusted to life in Bexhill-on-Sea. His 'thoughts' on this subject are what follows.

Welcome to Oliver's Tale

1. I've Arrived

Hello, Oliver here.

I am living in Bexhill with a right couple of Charlies. How do I know it's Bexhill? Because we all have a sleep in the afternoon, that's how. I think I'm too young to live in Bexhill really.

I live with a couple of people who don't seem to have much idea about me at all. One of them is a great big hairy chap with a ginger beard. The other one has a lovely soft touch when she rubs her hand over my coat.

I do pretty much as I please here and go where I like. There are a couple of beds which are just right for a nap and a lot of big windowsills where I can sit and watch what's going on outside in my territory. On sunny days, when the windows are open, I'm able to go straight in and out of the garden, which is jolly handy because I don't have to wait for the doors to be opened.

For a bit of real fun, I would like to try going out of an upstairs window, but I haven't found the stairs yet. I suppose they must be in one of the cupboards in the hall. Come to think of it, we all sleep downstairs in this house, but I guess that's because the other two are too old to go upstairs to bed.

The food here is quite good and I've got a couple of tricks to get more if I want it. If I think they are going out and they want me to come in, I nip outside when they're not looking because then they come looking for me shaking the biscuit packet.

The other good wheeze is in the evening when they come home at different times. The first one home gives me my food in my dish which I then polish off as quickly as I can and I lick the bowl out until it is spotless. Then, when the other Charlie comes home, I sit by my bowl and get it filled again. Bingo! Hope they don't work that one out. They shouldn't do because I think they are a bit thick. Only problem is, I can't always manage the second bowlful.

Out in the garden I've had a bit of trouble with a couple of ginger cats. I had a proper dust up with one of them in his garden. Bloody nose I got. I've also got a nasty scratch on my ear but I'm not letting on how that got there or where I was when I got it. Best bit is when one of the ginger chaps is giving me trouble in my garden if Old Beardy is home. He chases them off. Funniest thing you ever did see. Like last night, for example. There I was having a bit of a shouting match with one of the gingers when all of a sudden, Old Beardy goes flying past me with a saucepan in his hand. Blimey, I thought, he's going to bash him over the head with it, this should be good. Turned out, it was full of water and ginger got a bit damp.

Guess what? They only went shopping and got me a scratching mat. How do I know it's a scratching mat? Because Beardy went and tried to show me how to use it! He did! Thank heavens I already had some idea of how to use a litter tray. On second thoughts, that could have been a real laugh.

Anyway, back to this mat thing. Well, they were dead keen for me to use it you see, they made that quite obvious. So I didn't. Well, if they are that keen for you to do something then you don't, do you? What I actually do is use it quietly when they aren't looking. That was fine until the other day when I didn't hear Old Beardy come into the room. There I was, caught red pawed. You should have seen the fuss he made of me.

I must go now because Old Beardy is home this afternoon so if I can get a bowl of food out of him, then I might be able to get some more from the other one when she gets home. They never seem to know what the other one is doing.

Bye for now,
Oliver

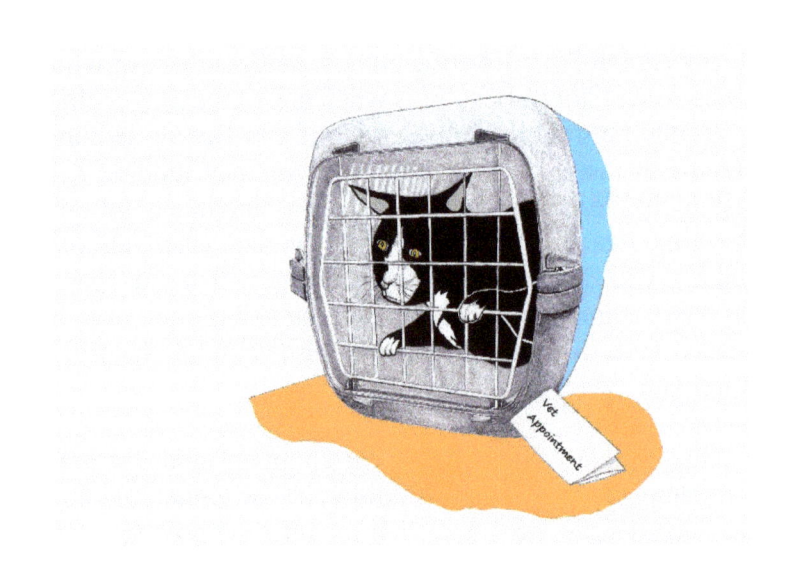

2. The Dreaded Box

Hello, Oliver here.

They've got a box. I have to go in it. A shiver goes down my spine just thinking about it. Any trip in the box usually ends up with me having to see a man with a big needle in a house that smells of disinfectant. All the way there and all the way back they're saying, "It's all right Ollie, you'll be OK." Well, if that's their idea of me being OK, then I'd hate to be around when things aren't OK.

We had a visitor. A tramp I think he was. Stinker they called him. Boy, what a good name for him. Sometimes he stayed and sometimes he didn't. Trouble was, sometimes he used his tray and sometimes he didn't. Sometimes he 'did it' in the tray and sometimes he didn't. And he had three trays to my one. And when he didn't use one of his three trays, he 'did it' anywhere. No manners at all. Terrible habit. I couldn't believe that they kept letting him come in. It got to the point where I tried to show him the correct procedure before I got the blame for something that was where it shouldn't be. I showed him: quick scratch in the tray, hop in, 'do it,' build a sandcastle over the top as a feature and hop out again. Stinker never quite got it though. Don't think he was quite all there. Few biscuits short of a full packet, if you know what I mean? I guess that's why he got on so well with Old Beardy and the other one.

He came unstuck in the end though. Must have been bad. Never did see what he did. He turned up here one Saturday evening for his dinner just as I was having mine. Chicken in jelly I think it was. Anyway, all of a sudden Old Beardy went charging out the door carrying 'The Box' and Stinker was inside. Well, about half an hour later, back came Beardy with 'The Box', and it was empty. I don't know what Stinker did wrong, but I hope I don't ever make the same mistake.

I thought I might have done last Saturday. They had given me something to eat that didn't agree with me. I couldn't face my breakfast on Saturday morning. Tummy churning. Home came Beardy and the fun started. All of a sudden, I felt both ends about to go. I got to the litter tray just in time. Whoosh! Whole body emptied. What a pong! Couldn't face hanging around to build sandcastles so I settled down to recover behind the armchairs. Home came the other one and they saw what had happened. Next thing you know, there's Old Beardy looking at me with that glint in his eye. And I recognise that glint in his eye now. Sure enough, there's ' The Box ' on the chair. Quick sticks, I'm out of here, round the chair and making a bid for the door

5

with Beardy close behind, but he's already closed the door. So, I opt for plan B, quick 180 degrees back between his legs and a swift dive under the table. It's worked before. Didn't make the table. He grabbed me round my middle. Couldn't really miss could he? There's plenty to grab.

So, that's it then. That's what Stinker must have done. Don't make a mess like that on a Saturday otherwise that's your lot. One trip to the disinfectant house on an empty tummy and that'll be my lot. Well, we saw the man with the big needles, and he also stuck what felt like a pencil up my bum. He wouldn't have done that if he had seen the deposit I'd just made in my tray, but they obviously hadn't told him. However, I was allowed to go home again. Can you believe it? They must have had second thoughts and decided to give me another chance. That wasn't the end of it though. The two Charlies only decided to try and give me a tablet. Don't know where they got that idea from but honestly, you should have seen them. Both of them it took. I still won though. I put it under my tongue and spat it out in the hall. They didn't try that again. The best bit is, I am feeling much better now, and my tummy has settled down. That's without any more of their daft silly tablets.

Bye for now,
Oliver

3. *I Nearly Got The Boot*

Hello, Oliver here.

Boy what an atmosphere there is in our house at the moment, Old Beardy has really got the hump with me. It all happened last night just after dinner. They gave me some kind of meat in gravy, my favourite. In fact, any kind of meat in gravy is my favourite. I like to lick the bowl round and usually end up with a bit on the end of my nose and some on the whiskers under my chin. Just like Old Beardy when he eats his Sunday dinner.

Anyway, they only give me one bowlful for dinner these days and I really did fancy some more gravy. So, while they had their dinner I went outside and sat on the top of the wall to try and think of a plan. They shut me out until they had finished their dinner and then opened the door, so I jumped down off the wall, landed a bit hard, and popped back indoors.

Well, I limped past them, but they didn't take much notice. Old Beardy was saying something about how pleased he was to have £50 put by to get his motorcycle boots back from the repairers. As they hadn't noticed my 'limp' the first time, I limped past them again. Should have seen them this time. Big fuss. Couldn't leave me alone. Didn't fill my bowl again though, oh no. This fuss went on for about an hour, so I thought I would lay it on a bit thick. Started squawking a bit if you know what I mean? That certainly got a reaction.

Out of the room went Old Beardy and back comes some more gravy? Wrong. Back came Old Beardy with ' The Box'. Hang on fellas, I think to myself, I was only kidding. Too late! I was bundled straight into the box. Before I knew it, we're off down the road in the car. We can't be going to see the man with the big needles this time, it must be way past his bedtime. Wrong again.

The man with the big needles seemed to be expecting us. I couldn't believe it. Well, he pulled me this way and he pulled me that way and he pushed me here and he pushed me there. I kept quiet. I'm not that silly. If I made out it hurt now, I'd be sure to get a needle. He says I'm a fraud and gives me a great big needle anyway. Rotten chap. Just because I must have got him out of bed.

Old Beardy paid up and off we went, with him muttering something about that being a big hole in twenty quid. What about the big hole in my neck where that needle went, eh? Funny there's no mention of that. Back in the car and Old Beardy is still muttering something about bang goes his motorbike boots and the only boot we're likely to see this week is the one he's going to put up my backside. Charming!

We got back home, and I didn't fancy a boot up my backside so as soon as I got out of the box I went into the back room and settled down behind the piano. He can't reach me there. Came after me, he did, prattling on about how he's not spending the thick end of twenty quid for me to go and be anti-social. Poked me up the bum with something so I shot off into the kitchen and waited by the back door. In he came, picked me up and carried me into the room where the other one is watching the television. Is he thick or what? If I had wanted to be in the same room as them, I would have walked in there myself. I certainly didn't need him to carry me. Then came the best bit of all. You won't believe this. He went out of the room, came back in, and guess what he's got? Meat in gravy - that's what.

After all that, I just glared at him, I don't want it now, thank you. Yes, there's definitely an atmosphere in our house at the moment.

Bye for now,
Oliver

4. I've Had A Busy Week

Hello, Oliver here.

Boy what a week I've had. Saw off one of the Ginger Chaps out in the garden, reorganized my sleeping arrangements indoors and found out Old Beardy is only half the man I thought he was.

Early one evening, I was sitting by the back door, which was open, waiting for Old Beardy to come home from work. I was also hoping the other Charlie would dish up my dinner. Then, one of the Ginger Chaps shows up, bold as brass, trying to sneak through my garden. Well, Beardy wasn't home to see him off with a saucepan and it was no good expecting the other Charlie to deal with it, her being a girlie and all that, so I thought I'd deal with it myself. I nipped outside double quick and stood up to him I did, nose to nose, barely a whisker between us. I shouted at him at the top of my voice. Got the message he did, turned and ran back up the path with me hot on his heels. We got to the corner by the compost bin, good place for him, and he must have lost his footing because suddenly there he was lying on his back, paws in the air. Stood over him I did, pinned him down. Out came the Charlie from indoors clapping and shouting and telling me to let him go, so I did. Straight across the road he went and hid under a car. Well, that wasn't far enough for me, so after him I went, and we started shouting in the street. Told to leave him alone I was, so I did. Off up the road he ran and I haven't seen him since. Besides, I didn't want to miss my dinner.

Now, ever since I've lived here it has been the same routine every night at bedtime. A few biscuits in my bowl for my supper and then it's "Night, night, Ollie, see you in the morning." The lounge door is shut and that's where I have to stay, all alone, until morning. Well, halfway through the other night, a big thunderstorm blew up, flashing and banging about. I could still hear Old Beardy snoring his head off in the bedroom but all of a sudden the lounge door burst open and the other Charlie came dashing in, picked me up, gave me a quick cuddle and carried me back into the bedroom where I spent the rest of the night on the bottom of her bed because she doesn't like thunderstorms.

Later that day, I got to thinking. Surely it would be a good idea if I spent every night sleeping at the bottom of her bed, then I would always be there if I was needed? So, now, as soon as I hear "bedtime Ollie," I'm in the bedroom before they are. They haven't thrown me out yet so they must be pleased to have me in there. Not so much Old Beardy but I think the other one likes me being there. I think she's a big old Softy really. Couldn't help wondering why Old Beardy isn't any use to her in the bedroom though.

Think I found out a couple of days later. I've had my eye on a tasty little number that sits on top of a gatepost over the road, multi-coloured she is, a dear little thing. Well, Old Beardy had seen me eyeing her up and he told me to forget it as I've been 'muted' or something, which is supposed to keep me quiet in that department. Only chance I've got of pleasing her, he says, is if I do what most of the other old boys in our street probably do and have a 'Niagara' tablet. I think that's what he said. Says he will ask the vet, (who's he?), if there is any such thing as 'Niagara' tablets for cats. Then he changes his mind and says, "Bearing in mind your attitude to tablet taking perhaps you'd better forget it, besides, I don't think you're fully equipped down below anyway." I just looked at him in amazement. Look here Buster, I thought, how come I was needed in the bedroom when we had that thunderstorm eh? You obviously didn't have the balls for that. Then the penny dropped and I was on to him. And how come you know so much about these 'Niagara' tablets anyway? Well, he hasn't spoken to me since, so that proves it. Old Beardy must be more muted than I am!

See you soon,
Oliver

5. The Lost Ball

Oliver here,

I lost my ball. I've got a small green ball which I really enjoy knocking around the room, dribbling it up the hall and best of all, chasing it around the kitchen as that's a tiled floor, so I can really get the ball to move in there. I also like to poke it under things and then try to get it back. Sometimes I can't quite reach it though.

The other morning, just after breakfast, I knocked it a bit hard and it disappeared under the bureau. Try as I might, I couldn't get it back. Old Softy realised I'd lost it but said she didn't have time to look for it or she would be late for work, or something. Just as she was going out the door, Old Beardy came out from the bedroom. What a sight. "See you tonight," Softie shouts, followed by, "have a look for

Oliver's ball will you, I think he's lost it." "Great," says Old Beardy as he looked down at me, "Come on then, let's get this over and done with before I do anything else." Into the lounge we went and he started. Up in the air went the first armchair, up in the air went the second armchair, then it was the settee, followed by the rug by the fireplace.

"What have you done with it this time Oliver?" He asked as he went down on his hands and knees again. All the way round the room he went, shouting out occasionally "not under the sideboard, not under the bureau." I think it is, I say to myself. Up on to his feet again, he started to look in the hall. I hear the cupboard doors banging and dash out after him to see if I can catch a glimpse of the stairs. Too late, he's gone into the bedroom. Up in the air the first bed went, then the second, then he's down on all fours again and all around the room he went, with me watching him from the hall.

Out he came, still on all fours, to make his way into the back room. He paused for a moment and looked at me, his hair absolutely everywhere, like a big shaggy dog, his face the colour of beetroot and said, "I really needed all this with a head like I've got this morning." Pity its empty, I think to myself. I sat and watched his backside wobble gently from side to side as he made his way into the back room with his pyjama trousers sliding slowly towards the point of no return, just saved by a swift hand as he turned the corner.

Round the room he went, "Not under the chairs or behind the piano," he shouts. No, I still think it's under the bureau, I say to myself. He appeared again, up on his feet this time. He checked out their toilet and then their bathroom and then he went into the kitchen. Different approach for this room as he didn't go down on all fours but bent over double instead and went around bobbing up and down, looking here, there and everywhere. It reminded me of a programme they watch on the television, ' Monkey World ' I think it's called.

    He finally gave up. "I can't find it anywhere," he said, "I suppose I will have to buy you another one." I looked up at him. I bet you half a tin of meat in gravy, that Old Softy finds it when she gets home from work tonight. "I'm off for a bath," he said. That will make it rain, I thought, as I settled down for a nap.
    In the evening, Softy eventually arrived home. "Hello, I'm home," she shouted as she opened the back door. "Have you found Ollie's ball?" she asked Beardy, "I've looked everywhere, and I couldn't find it," he replied. "You can't have looked everywhere otherwise you would have found it. I suppose I'll have to find it," she said as we all went into the lounge. I looked at the clock as she got down on her hands and knees. "It's not under the sideboard or the chairs. What about the bureau? Here it is Ollie," she shouted as she jumped to her feet with a smile and handed the ball to Old Beardy, who stood there with his mouth wide open. Wow! How about that then? Twenty-eight seconds. That's got to be a record. She's never beaten half a minute before. I didn't even look at Beardy as I walked straight past him and followed Softy into the kitchen to collect my winnings.

See you soon,
Oliver

6. *I Only Sneezed*

Hello, Oliver here.

I've been a bit under the weather again, had a bit of a cold. Not too much of a problem as I see it, because I feel OK otherwise and I'm not off my food or anything. Only thing is I've been sneezing occasionally. Sometimes I sneeze in the daytime and then also at night. That's the awkward bit. Now that I sleep in the bedroom with Old Beardy and Softy, my sneezing has caused a bit of trouble.

    The other night, because I was feeling a bit rough, I settled down to sleep a bit higher up Softy's bed, instead of at the bottom of the bed, and I was right between the two of them. The beds are quite close together. Old Beardy is quite long when he's lying down and he usually slips further and further down the bed as the night progresses. By the morning, he can be overhanging the bottom of the bed by a full two feet, if you know what I mean?

Now, it just so happened that when I sneezed, I must have been facing Beardy, and as he had slipped down the bed a bit, it meant that I was in line with his left ear. Not that anyone has ever seen his left ear, or the right one come to that, buried under all that hair and fuzz as they are. Not like me, I like to keep my ears sticking out in the fresh air otherwise my hair would make them tickle.

Anyway, all I did was sneeze. What a commotion that caused. Up sat Old Beardy and on came the light. Not a pretty sight. "Every time he sneezes it wakes me up," he said. If you're talking about me, the name is Oliver, I think to myself. "Whose idea was it for him to sleep in here with us anyway?" he went on. Well, as it happens it was mine, but it's not a good time to tell him that, so I just give him a blank look. Don't look at me, I can't remember, I think to myself. Softy is just starting to 'come to' as he goes on. "Four times he's sneezed tonight and he's woken me up every time." Can you believe it, he's actually been counting. "I'll only have had three hours sleep when I go to work, how can I work a long day on that?" he asks. Your days aren't any longer than anyone else's I think to myself. Softy tried a line of defence for our bed. "Oliver can't help having a bit of a cold," she said. "I will try and get him something to take when I go to the shops today." Good try. Off he went again. "That's all very well and good but it doesn't help me now, does it? Four times he's sneezed - 1 o'clock, 1.30, 2.10, and 2.30, and I've got to get up at half past three." Well, that did it. He's even keeping a note of the times. I've never heard anything so ridiculous in all my life and I'd had enough. I looked at him. Now look here Buster, if you don't pipe down jolly soon, I'm going to jump down off this bed and poop on the carpet and then you'll really have something to moan about. That did the trick. Off went the light & back down under the covers he went. Didn't make another sound.

Funny thing is though, all my food has tasted of garlic since then, I can't understand it.

Bye for now,
Oliver

7. I Go As I Like

Ollie here,

I used to live in Eastbourne before moving to Bexhill. I was very happy living in Eastbourne and didn't really see any need to move but it was kind of forced upon me. The toilet arrangements there were different to the toilet arrangements in Bexhill. In Eastbourne everyone used to 'go' outside and nothing was thought of it. I had a litter tray indoors just in case I needed to 'go' during the night, which was very rare, otherwise I would hang on until morning and 'go' outside just like everybody else.

When I moved to Bexhill, however, I wasn't allowed outside at all for some time, so I was forced to use a litter tray indoors all the time. During the daytime, I used to spend a lot of time sitting on the windowsills looking outside, either at the garden at the back or the garden at the front. When I was looking out of the front windows, I could see people walking up and down the street and some of them would be walking their dogs. Not a subject I like talking about too much. It became apparent to me that not only was I not allowed outside to 'go' but the dogs were not supposed to 'go' outside either. I could tell this by the fact that if one of them couldn't 'hang on' until he got back home and had to 'go' in the street then his owner would quickly pick it up, pop it in a bag and take it home with them.

Well, as time passed, I was allowed outside to explore my new surroundings but I always remembered to dash back inside if I needed to 'go'. Then funny things started to happen. First of all, my litter tray was moved and put by the back door. So I used it by the back door. Then it was placed just outside the back door. So I used it just outside the back door. Then it got tricky. I had a job finding it. It wasn't where it usually is at night and it wasn't by the back door, inside or out. I had to 'hang on'. Late in the day I saw the front door open and went to explore the porch. There it was. High up on a shelf. Could I get to it though, that was the question. I was getting desperate so I would have to try. There was a small gap just in front of the tray which I could possibly squeeze onto, so I jumped. Got the front half of my body straight onto the shelf and the back half followed, sort of running up the wall for the last bit and there I was, squeezed on to the shelf next to the tray. With my ears laid flat as possible and my head just gently brushing the shelf above, I climbed carefully into the tray and lowered my bottom for business. Only problem was my tail. Couldn't stick it up because of the shelf above. Not enough room behind so I had to curl it up over the side and then out and up to my left. The next question was, was I actually desperate enough to spend a penny in this position? Well, as you know, when it's a question of desperation versus position, desperation usually wins. Sure enough, as the relief started to flow through my tense, rigid body, I just looked straight ahead. My Mum told me as a little kitten:

"Son, if you ever have to 'do' anything at a great height, don't look down or you might feel dizzy." This must have been what she meant and it certainly wasn't the right time to feel dizzy. When I had finished, I very carefully climbed out of the tray and jumped down onto the floor. Success!

As I walked away, I glanced back up and pondered the thought, if I had slipped and the whole lot had come tumbling down, whose fault would it have been? Not mine, that's for sure. The tray was never put on the shelf again. No, they left it where it was in future, and covered it up in the daytime. So I would 'hang on'. I knew their bedtime would come before mine. For the next few days, I would use the tray first thing in the morning, when I heard them getting up, then 'hang on' until they were ready for bed in the evening and nip in quick when it was uncovered for the night. There was no way they would risk leaving the lid on at night after it had been on all day. They soon got fed up with those games though and I use the tray whenever I like now, night or day. We are just so much more civilised in Bexhill-on-Sea.

Bye for now,
Oliver

8. Trouble Cooking

Hello, Oliver here.

Old Beardy has got the hump. Got to spend some more money he has. Trouble with the cooker apparently. It's an all-electric cooker with a high-level grill. First of all it had a ring that wouldn't switch off. Then this week, the grill wouldn't work. Beardy said that with Christmas only three weeks away he knows exactly which week the oven will pack up. Got his Mum coming for Christmas dinner you see. I wonder what I will get for Christmas dinner. I hope it's like a Sunday dinner because if they are home on a Sunday they usually cook a chicken. Sunday is the only day I get a bit of what they are having for dinner and I love freshly cooked chicken. Softy says it's my Sunday treat. I wonder what she gives Old Beardy for his Sunday treat. Same as me I expect. Chicken.

Anyway, back to this cooker problem. Old Beardy has been out two afternoons this week looking for a new one. Cheapest he can find, knowing him. He says that the electrical shop in St. Leonards can get the same as we've got now, but don't have any in stock. The big store at Ravenside don't stock any all-electric cookers with a high-level grill but the shop in Bexhill has three. Beardy said there is probably a market for cookers with high level grills in Bexhill, as the residents don't like bending. Should suit him then, I thought. "If you want one with a timer," he said to Softy, "then you will have to have a double-oven cooker with the grill in the top oven, but then you'll have to bend lower to get to the main oven." There he goes again about bending. That'll be the day when I see him at the oven, I thought. Well, Softy couldn't decide which one to have so they turned and looked at me. "Which one shall we have Ollie?" asked Old Beardy. Great, I think to myself, he has finally realised which one of us has got the brains around here. Trouble is, before I can answer, Softy said, "If we have a double oven, we will have to have the top oven door open all the time the grill is on, and Oliver might pinch the sausages." "That's decided then," said Old Beardy, "a high-level grill it will have to be."

All this talk of Christmas and the pantomimes have already started in our house. I say house, but I still can't find the stairs. The other day, late in the afternoon, when there was just Old Beardy and me at home, he sat down in his recliner, poor old chap, to have a cup of tea and a piece of his Mum's cake. He says although Softy is a good cook, she can't make a cake quite like his Mum's. Pathetic! He's on dodgy ground there if you ask me.

Anyway, it was obvious that I wasn't getting any, so I went into the bedroom to see what I could get up to. I was just settling down for a good scratch, no I didn't have an itch, it wasn't my body I was scratching. Trouble was, Old Beardy must have heard me because I heard him get out of his chair and start coming up the hall. Quick as my chubby little legs would go, I dashed into the back room and hid behind the piano because I knew I would be in trouble. I had watched Beardy put the shelf back over the piano a few days earlier. He has to take the shelf down if he wants to get me out, so I thought I was pretty safe. In he came, saw where I was and said, "I don't know what you've been up to Oliver but you can jolly well stay there and think about it." Off he went and shut the door. One thing's for sure, I thought, he won't leave the door shut for long because I don't have a litter tray in the back room. That, in fact, is probably the only thing I can thank Stinker the tramp for. He had such an unreliable bottom that they never risk leaving me without access to a litter tray.

Sure enough, a little while later the door opened and in came Old Beardy. I nipped out from behind the piano and into the hall where he joined me, closing the door behind him. It was a bit gloomy because every door in the hall was shut. Just me and him. "That's got you out from behind the piano, now are you going to behave?" He watched as I went to each door to make sure that they were all properly shut and then I sat and looked at him. He then had to show off. Opening doors and going into rooms as he pleased, always closing the doors behind him. This won't last long, I thought, I still can't get to my litter tray. Sure enough, he left the lounge door open, so I went in. He ignored me for ages. I tried walking over to him but he still ignored me. Then he looked down at me and said, "Well, Oliver, are you going to behave?" I rolled over onto my back and looked up at him. "That's all right then," he said, rubbing my tummy. Well, I thought, Old Beardy has got to feed me tonight so I had better stay on good terms with him and after all, he will be at work tomorrow and I can do what I like again.

Bye for now,
Oliver

9. My First Christmas With Them

Hello, Oliver here.

Just thought I would let you know how my first Christmas with the two Charlies went.

Well, after all the fuss over the new cooker, we finally had it fitted the weekend before Christmas. Once it was connected up and working, Old Beardy and Softy disappeared off in his car for a couple of hours. When they returned, they had a tree inside the car. Very strange, I thought. Then it got better. They brought the tree indoors and stuck it in a pot in the lounge. Wouldn't have done that if I was a dog, I know. I've seen what those dogs do to trees. Awful! Decorated it all up they did with lights and hung balls from the branches. Great fun I had with those, tapping them from side to side.

Then came Christmas Eve. I sat on Softy's lap and we watched Old Beardy hang all the Christmas cards up. She's got the right idea there I thought. I also noticed a big 'chilly' looking bird lying on the work top in the kitchen with its head missing. I wonder if that's for me I thought. I couldn't have caught one that big. Old Beardy said a bird that size must be the 'Oliver' of the bird world. I wonder what he meant. We all had to go to bed early on Christmas Eve as we would all be getting up early in the morning. It can't be for Old Beardy to open his presents, I thought, as who would give him anything?

Christmas morning came and we did get up early just so Softy could get the bird, 'a turkey' they called it, into the oven. Sounded good to me. "Right," said Softy, "let's open the presents, we must do Oliver's first as he's got three." Looks like I might enjoy today after all, I thought, as she started to unwrap the first one. It was from a very good friend of Old Beardy, called Brenda. Softy is already onto him on that one. She said to him once before "It's funny how all your 'very good' friends seem to be women." He's definitely on a dodgy wicket there, but I think I'm going to like Brenda. More importantly, back to my present. It was quite a big ball with string sides and patches that smelt lovely. I had a good sniff of it and tapped it about a bit and then Softy started opening my next present. This one was from the two of them. I don't think I believe that.

It was a rather nice smelling Father Christmas. Are they kidding, do they really think I believe in Father Christmas? I ignored that one and waited for my last present. "Oh dear," said Softy as she unwrapped and opened the box. "I think I wasted my money here." See? I was right, these two presents were nothing to do with Old Beardy at all. "Look, just a few biscuits and a ping pong ball," she said as she threw the ball onto the floor. It looked OK to me though so I went to investigate. A ball that smelt of biscuit. Can't beat that, I thought as I gave it a nifty swipe. It shot across the room. No effort at all. I tested it up and down the hall, a brilliant bit of kit. I took it into the kitchen and tried it out on the hard floor. Slight tap and it was gone. Couldn't keep up with it. It wasn't a waste of money as far as I was concerned. They reckon it will help me lose weight trying to catch it. I'm not sure about that myself.

The morning soon passed with a visit from Softy's Mum and Dad, they didn't bring me anything. Then Beardy went and got his Mum. She didn't bring me anything either but I quite liked her. She's about the same size as Old Beardy but a different shape. She's much kinder looking as well. No sign of a ginger beard though, I had a good look. I suppose she must be his Mum if he says so. I wonder where she went wrong with Old Beardy. We all had that 'turkey' for dinner, Yippee, and 'they' washed it down with a bottle of 'happy juice'. They couldn't manage the pudding straight away so they collapsed into the armchairs. For the record, I could have managed a pudding but I wasn't offered one.

Beardy's Mum had a comfy looking lap so I jumped up onto that. She wasn't so sure but I knew she would see how lucky she was that I had chosen her by the end of the afternoon. They all settled down to watch a film on the television about little people, The Borrowers, it was called.

Rather amusing, I thought, judging by the size of Old Beardy and his Mum. I settled down on her lap and did my Beardy impression. That's where I stretch right out with my belly puffed up and pretend to be asleep. When the film had finished they decided they could squeeze their pudding in and then it was time for Beardy to take his Mum home because she couldn't manage any tea. I could and I did. Mind you, his Mum was jolly dodgy on her feet when she stood up. She blamed it on me. She said, "Your heavy Oliver has made my legs go dead." What a cheek! Never mind all those glasses of 'happy juice' she had with her dinner.

So that was the end of our Christmas Day. Beardy took his Mum home, Softy tidied up the kitchen and I had another game with my new, lightweight, biscuit smelling Ping Pong Ball.

Bye for now,
Oliver

10. What Did He Call Me?

Hello, Oliver here,

He called me a Pillock, Beardy did. Now that I'm allowed to sleep in the bedroom with them, I don't always bother. Once you're allowed to do something you don't, do you? It doesn't seem so much fun as doing the things you aren't supposed to. Besides, Old Beardy's snoring keeps me awake so I usually sleep on a chair in the lounge these days. l think Softy misses me sleeping on her bed though because I have noticed she leaves the door open.

Anyway, back to this Pillock business. It happened the other night. Beardy went to bed early, as he often does, and Softy stayed up with me for a while. When it got quite late,

30

she went to bed as well so I sat by the back door looking through the glass. It was all quiet for a while and then I saw something move outside. I shouted at it, but it didn't go away, so I shouted even louder. It stayed there looking at me so I shouted and screamed at the top of my voice. All of a sudden, in came Softy from the bedroom. "What's all the noise about Ollie?" I just kept screaming my head off. Then in came Old Beardy. "What's going on?" he said to Softy. "There must be something outside," she replied. They bundled me into the hall and closed the kitchen door as Old Beardy went running outside with his torch. A few minutes later and he's back. "There's nothing out there Oliver, you must have been looking at your reflection in the glass, you Pillock." What a cheek! Well, I don't think it's me who's the Pillock, I thought, as I watched him go back to bed. You're the one who's just been round the garden in your underpants.

He seems to have been rude to me a lot lately but Softy always comes to my defence. She got him a good one when he was rude about my bird catching ability. Softy likes to feed the birds in the mornings and I like to watch them through the window. Sometimes she puts pieces of bread on the back lawn and then lets me out to chase the birds. Good exercise for me, she says. Well, it turns out that Old Beardy has been watching me from behind the net curtains and he finds it hilarious because once I'm in the garden the birds don't come down to feed anymore. He says he's seen me trying to hide behind the flowerpots on the patio but I'm so wide, the birds can see my body sticking out each side of the pot. Then, when I tried a different approach he got really nasty. I tried lying down on the ground under the tree. He said, "You dimwit Ollie, the birds can still see you because there aren't any leaves on the tree at this time of year." Then do you know what he said? "Still, Gatwick have been on the phone and asked us if we could get you to spread out in the back garden every day. Apparently, the pilots of the Jumbos use you as a marker when they come back across the channel and turn left over Bexhill heading for Gatwick." What a nasty piece of work. Trouble was, Softy heard what he said and got him back. She said, "Well, I wasn't going to mention it but, last summer I had Heathrow on the phone asking if I could get you to wear a shirt when you mow the lawn because the sun was reflecting off your tummy, dazzling the pilots and before they knew it they were coming in to land at Stansted." Wow, you should have seen his face. Don't think I'll be getting any more trouble from him when Softy is around.

Bye for now,
Oliver

11. Mice's

Hello, Oliver here.

I caught a mouse I did. It was the other night just after I'd had my dinner. Well, some of my dinner as I always save a bit for later. Softy said, "Oh look, Ollie wants to have a game with his ball but I'm too busy to play with him tonight." Apparently, she had got an early start in the morning because she had to travel to Dorking, (I think that's what she called it), to work every day this week. "Two hours each way," she said, "so every night this week will have to be an early night."

Old Beardy was his usual miserable self after already having had a bad day so he didn't want to play with me either, so I went outside for a while. A bit later on, the back door opened, "Goodnight Ollie, it's 8.15 and I'm off to bed," Beardy says as I nip past him and through into the lounge. He followed me in to say goodnight. "HE'S GOT A MOUSE," he shouts. "WHAT?" screams Softy from the kitchen as she leapt up onto a chair. "Oliver's caught a mouse," says Beardy followed by "Oh, no, now he's gone and lost it." Well, yes, I had caught a mouse - so that showed them. All the ridicule I've had to put up with since I came to live in Bexhill about being too fat and too slow to catch anything. So now I had proved them wrong. Only trouble was, Old Beardy's shouting had distracted me and the little mouse had run off under one of the armchairs to hide. That did it for me. I'm afraid to say I got the hump and I went and sat by the back door again. Mind you, Softy did look funny standing on top of the chair as I passed her in the kitchen.

Old Beardy didn't have much of a clue about finding the mouse though. He overturned the chairs and the settee. (I know that because he was giving Softy a running commentary as he went). And then he came and got me. "Come on Oliver, you brought the mouse in here so you can jolly well help me find it," he said as he marched me back into the lounge.

Well, I looked at the mess he had made and went and sat on the windowsill behind the curtain. He lost it for me, I thought, so he can jolly well find it. I heard him move the coffee table back from the wall "HERE IT IS - THERE IT GOES," he shouts as the little mouse gave him the slip again. I would like to point out at this stage that I do not care much for Old Beardy when he starts shouting, nor do I like some of the language he uses when his face begins to turn purple.

"Come in here and help me," he said to Softy "I'm like a one-man band in here trying to catch this thing. While you're at it," he goes on, "turn all the lights on so we can see what we're doing and bring an old ice-cream tub with a lid that we can put the mouse in when we catch it." I couldn't help noticing that he used the words "when we catch it." He had been chasing the mouse for half an hour by now and there appeared to be a note of bitter determination in his voice. It was obviously going to be a fight to the bitter end. Question was, who would win? To her credit, Softy did come into the lounge to assist as they pulled units away from the wall, all to no avail.

After a while they gave up. "Come on Ollie, just give us a clue," said Old Beardy. This had been going on for almost an hour by now and, to be honest, I was beginning to wish Beardy would just go to bed so I could have some peace and quiet. I jumped down from the windowsill and went over to the tall units in the comer where Softy keeps her best china. I had a sniff at the carpet and tried to peer behind them and then walked away again. "Ollie says the mouse is behind here," said Beardy as he started to pull the first unit away from the wall. "Hadn't we better take the china out before you move it?" asked Softy anxiously. "No, it'll be all right. There he is, I can see him," said Beardy as he gets the ice-cream tub at the ready. "Don't you let him anywhere near me," shouts Softy, backing away. "It's OK, I've got him," said Beardy dropping the little chap into the tub followed swiftly by the lid. "I will just pop him outside and then we will tidy up," he said as he disappeared out of the back door.

I don't know what he did with the mouse but I didn't see it again. They did have a tidy up and we all got to bed about a quarter to ten. At least that's what Old Beardy said the time was because he wasn't very happy about it being so late. "Fancy Oliver catching something," said Softy as she snuggled down under the covers. "Yes," replied Beardy "It must have been a pretty dozy mouse to be caught by him." Not half as dozy as you, I thought, I had to show you it was behind the wall unit otherwise you never would have caught it.

Bye for now,
Oliver

12. Ugly Mug

Hello, Oliver here.

We've had a bit of a rumpus recently and as usual it was Old Beardy's fault. It all started on Sunday. I always know when it is Sunday because Old Beardy gets up first after a bit of a lie in by his standards and gives me my breakfast. This is followed shortly afterwards by Softy emerging from the bedroom, rubbing her eyes, and muttering something like "Why on earth do we have to get up so early on a Sunday? It's not even 7 O'clock yet." To which Beardy replies.... .... He wouldn't risk it.

Softy was off out for the day to help a Brass Band in a competition. She had spent every evening last week practicing. This is where Softy goes into the back room with a big shiny instrument and Beardy and I go as fast as we can into the front room, closing all the doors behind us, and he turns the television up loud. With Softy gone for the day, Old Beardy had to get his own dinner and he gave me a few biscuits as a treat. I usually get some fresh chicken for my treat on a Sunday but, as there was no sign of Softy coming home yet, I was quite happy with a few biscuits.

All of a sudden, as soon as Old Beardy had finished his dinner, up he jumped and said, "Right, that's it Ollie, I've had enough of this," takes off his shirt and disappears into the bathroom with a big pair of scissors. Whatever can be wrong? What is he going to do? I thought, as I settled down to wait for him in the hall. He was in there quite a while, although I'm not sure how long as we don't have a clock in the hall. Just nodding off I was when the bathroom door burst open and there he was. Good Lord! Never seen anything like it. I wasn't prepared for this. He went in with a good ten or twelve inches of beard and now it was nearly all gone. He was all face and double chin. What an Ugly Mug. Whatever will Softy say? I expect she will make him put it back on. Can't let him outside looking like that or he will frighten the neighbours. Home came Softy and she said, "I do like your beard, you have made a good job of it this time," as she stroked his chin. Well, either she needs glasses, I've got wax in my ears and misheard her, or she wasn't telling the truth. As Old Beardy found out a few days later, the truth hurts.

I was sitting on the back door mat, with the door open listening to Softy telling Beardy about her day at work as they were eating their dinner. Softy works with several other ladies and a couple of men at a place where they all sit in a line and pay out lots of money to the customers. All their customers must be happy then. On this particular day she had been sat next to a lady who is rather keen to get herself a man with whom she can form a long-term, deep and meaningful relationship, Softy told Beardy. "I know all about those relationships," says Beardy. "That's where the girl gets herself a chap and he spends the rest of his life doing as he's told." "Shut up and listen," barked Softy. So he did. That sounded meaningful to me, I thought, as I watched a seagull fly over our garden. Softy had served a rather good-looking young man that afternoon and, after he had gone, her colleague had said "he was nice, pity he was married." "Is that the kind of chap you would like?" Softy had enquired. "Well, you want something nice to look at," her colleague had replied. "Looks aren't everything," Softy had said, "After all, I'm happy with my chap." CRASH! went Beardy's knife and fork as they hit the plate and he nearly choked on his mashed potato. "Thanks a lot," he spluttered, "That says a lot for me then." "No, no, no, you have got it all wrong," said Softy, "l didn't mean it like that."

Funny how it's always his fault for being upset after she's insulted him, I thought, as I watched a squirrel dash along the top of our garden wall. Well, Beardy went to bed even earlier than usual that night as I got myself comfy on Softy's lap. "I think I've upset your Dad, Ollie," she said. He's no relative of mine, I thought, as I rolled over onto my back. "He took it all the wrong way," she said as she stroked me under my chin. That's the idea, I thought to myself, you stick with me because I've only got one chin.

Bye for now,
Oliver

13. Beardy's Bikes

Hello, Oliver here.

Have I told you about Old Beardy and his motorbikes? Apparently, in his younger days, he used to have just one motorbike which he rode all year round and was classed as a motorcyclist. Now, he classes himself as a motorcycle enthusiast because, he says, "If you call yourself an enthusiast of something then you can have more than one of them."

Sounds like Softy is being conned on this one. Yes, he has got more than one bike, he hardly ever rides them, and they stay, polished up, under dust sheets in the garage. I don't understand it either. Just a great big wheeze to have more toys if you ask me.

I sometimes go into the garage when he is tinkering with his motorbikes because I like to have a good pull on the carpet with my claws. Yes, I did say carpet. Lino for some of the rooms indoors and carpet for the garage. As soon as he gets a bike out onto the drive to start it up though, I'm off, straight round to the back garden as fast as I can. I don't like the noise you see. Besides, he's not getting me on the back of one of those things. In fact, I don't think anyone goes on the back. Do you blame them? Almost wished I had gone with him yesterday though. I got the feeling something was going on when I watched Softy getting things together in the kitchen. Must be going for one of their days out I thought. Picnic time. Softy went into the bedroom as Old Beardy started taking bags outside to his motorbike parked on the drive. Might get a treat before he goes, I thought, so I started licking my bowl out ready. I heard a kind of slippery, crinkly sound and looked into the hall. I nearly pooped myself on the spot. Coming up the hall was some kind of creature. It was about the size of Softy, completely black, had two arms and legs and a dome at the top. There was what looked like a window on the front of the dome and the creature appeared to be waving an arm at me. The slippery, crinkly sound was coming from it as it walked. I could hear a muffled sound as if it was talking to me. I heard it say something like "My, My Ollie." I was scared stiff and went and hid in the lounge. I heard it go out of the front door and a little while later Beardy came in and put some biscuits down for me. "There you go Ollie," he said, "just off out for a few hours while the sun is shining. Don't you want your biscuits?" He must be joking I thought. Didn't he see that monster?

Well, after he had gone, I was too scared to look for Softy and I certainly didn't feel like eating anything. A few hours later I heard a key in the front door and had a look through the frosted glass. Hell's Bells, it was the monster coming back in. I ran and hid behind the settee. Then I heard Old Beardy come in the door. One thing about him is, he does always call out to me as he's opening the door so I know it's him. I stayed behind the settee though because I knew the monster had come in just before him. Beardy came looking for me saying, "What's up Ollie? You haven't touched your biscuits." Well, he was just making a fuss of me when I saw Softy come out of the bedroom. She must have gone back to bed after he had gone out and only just got up.

Things settled down a bit in the afternoon as we all sat down to watch the Formula 1 Grand Prix on the television. I got up onto Softy's lap to watch and after about ten minutes we are usually both fast asleep. I looked around the room just before I nodded off and spotted the gloves over the radiator and the jackets and trousers just in front. I looked at Old Beardy and thought, I don't know where you went this morning but the sun wasn't out when you got there then.

Bye for now,
Oliver

14. It's Curtains For Beardy

Hello, Oliver here.

Old Beardy has been doing a bit of B.I Y. Bodge It Yourself. Softy started it off by saying, "I think I am going to buy a door curtain for the back door because I can feel a draught when I'm standing at the sink." "Can you afford it?" asked Beardy. "Well, there are lots of Sales on at the moment and I would just like to go and buy something in the Sales and save some money," Softy replied. Beardy offered some of his typical logic. Look out, I thought. "Where?" he says, "is the sense in buying a curtain in a Sale when you will then have to buy a rail and a length of batten to put it on?" The look she gave him meant he was facing a heavy defeat, yet again, so he beat a hasty retreat with, "OK, if you can get a curtain rail and a length of batten, I will put it up for you." So, with that, Softy went off to the shops while Beardy settled back into his recliner to read his motorcycle paper and I settled down for a sleep.

Lunchtime arrived and back came Softy. Old Beardy looked up from behind his paper. "Any luck?" he asked. "Nobody does door curtains these days," she replied. "I suppose everybody has double glazed doors so they don't need them." A look of relief came over Old Beardy's face which was quickly ruined by Softy saying, "Never mind, I've got a couple more shops that I can try this afternoon."

Unfortunately for Old Beardy, the afternoon was more fruitful for Softy and by the evening we had a curtain and a rail. No length of batten though. Beardy was sure he would need a length of batten due to the back door being in a recess. This is not sounding very good I thought. Too technical for him, I was sure. Too late to go back to the shops for the missing batten so Old Beardy said "Not to worry. I will have a go at putting the curtain up tomorrow while you're at work and I will have to improvise for any bits I haven't got." Bodge it, I thought. He always manages his best Bodges when he is on his own.

Next day, with Softy at work, I settled down in the hall where I can see the front door where Beardy will go out to the garage to get his tools, the back door where Beardy will be trying to hang the curtain, and the hall. This should be good, I thought. Old Beardy got all his tools together, drill, screwdrivers, saw, screws, nails and hammer. Funny how every job needs a hammer, I thought. Then he started looking for a length of wood he could use as a batten. He looked in the two cupboards in the hall, no luck, then the airing cupboard, "Just the job," he said, coming back for his hammer. Unfortunately for Softy, we had watched a film the previous weekend called 'The Great Escape.' The men in the film needed some wood and they just ripped it out of the buildings, floorboards, joists, cupboards and beds and people like Beardy get ideas from films. Softy's airing cupboard has shelves made up of lengths of battens crisscrossing around the hot water tank. Now it was a batten short. The lunatic!

Well, it was all a big anti-climax. Holes were drilled, screws were screwed and the curtain was up. That's that then, I thought, as I headed for the back door. I don't believe it but he's actually done it. "Want to go out Ollie?" asked Beardy "Hold on and I'll open the door for you." Yes, he did open the door. It opened a whole six inches before it struck the batten. "I don't believe it," said Beardy. I do, I thought, as I sat back down to watch. Down it all came again. Now for Plan B. A piece of batten each side of the doorway with the rail passing through the doorway in mid-air. The result? Door opened with the rail rubbing along the top of the door. Down it all came again. Now for Plan C. Followed by Plans D, E and F. By which time two more slats were missing from the airing cupboard so it is likely Softy will overload the shelves in there one day.

Just in the nick of time we were all tidied up as Softy came home from work. "Curtain is up," said Beardy "But it doesn't move very easily because the hooks seem to act like a brake." "What have you gone and done now?" asked Softy "I will phone my Auntie Jean because she knows all about curtains." Off she went into the hall to use the telephone. Two minutes later, back came Softy, gets the furniture polish out, sprays the curtain rail and the curtain whizzes backwards and forwards. "See, I knew my Auntie Jean would know what was wrong, can't you do anything right?" said Softy, as Beardy stood there with his mouth hanging wide open.

Bye for now,
Oliver

15. Old Beardy Must Have Retired

Hello, Oliver here.

I can't quite understand it but Old Beardy seems to be spending a lot of time at home with me these days, I think he must have retired.

Since Christmas, which was over two months ago now, he has only worked the day after Boxing Day, New Year's Eve, one full week in January and just four days in February. Very strange, if you ask me, but then that's him all over. I guess he's retired and only goes back to help out from time to time when they are desperate - really desperate. Mind you, he may just be on strike because he has been talking a lot about his firm going on strike lately. Apparently, Old Beardy and all his work mates think they should be paid more money so the answer to this is a strike. From what I can understand, a strike is where Beardy and his mates all stay at home instead of going to work and that way, they don't get any money at all. I know, don't ask me where the logic is in that. Now you can see what I have to put up with.

    The day after Boxing Day, when he came home from work, he didn't look very well and apart from being a couple of hours late he was walking a bit funny. Pub I thought, and there's him always going on about how he doesn't drink. Trouble was he kept staggering about and groaning for the next few days. Hangover, I thought. He went back to work on New Year's Eve and the same thing happened again, he came staggering home late. Softy was on to him this time. "You're late," she said. "I know," he replied "I've had a terrible day, my van wouldn't start, it took them three hours to find me another van and by the time I got back to the office everyone else had gone home." Wow, what a whopper, I thought, where's the proof? Got away with it he did, she believed him.

    The day after New Year's Day he went off to work again but came home about half an hour later. Changed his mind he had, decided to go and see the Doctor instead. Not a subject I'm too keen on. I think Old Beardy has got the same Doctor as me because he doesn't like having his temperature taken either. The Doctor diagnosed strained groin muscles and he spent the next three weeks at home with me. How on earth could he have strained his groin muscles? I've yet to see the day when he rushes anywhere.

Well, after the three weeks were up, he went back to work but only lasted a week. Things were looking dodgy by the Friday but I won't tell you which things. He came home walking funny again, and said, "Golly Ollie, you should see what's happened now, it's something you're never likely to get," and went and sat in the bath. Something I'm never likely to get? I thought, whatever can he mean?

Back to the Doctor he went and then had another three weeks at home with me. Getting fed up with this I was and do you know what he had wrong this time? An infection! What was all that he had said about me not being able to have the same problem? BALLS I thought, I've had an infection before. Three weeks later, off he goes back to work again and only lasts four days this time. For goodness' sake, what's he going to come up with this time? Now it starts to get interesting. The Doctor has given up on him, you see, says he will have to go to the hospital and have 'them' looked at by a specialist. Them? So now we're waiting. Beardy's got the wind up. He doesn't like the thought of specialists, hospitals and knives.

Ahh! I've waited a long time for this. I can remember being in the same situation myself when I was about two years old. Justice at last.

Bye for now,
Oliver

16. It's A Funny Walk

Hello, Oliver here.

It's turning into another of those weeks. Old Beardy is still at home all the time with his funny walk and Softy is home this week as well. That worried me a bit. It can be dodgy when they are both at home. I can cope with one of them but when the two of them are together, they can play up a bit.

Sunday evening Softy said, "We must Front-Line Ollie tonight, so you hold him while I do it." Here we go, I thought. Beardy thinks this is funny. He caught me unawares because I was having a nice nap on Softy's lap when all this started so he managed to pick me up before I could do a runner. Softy gets what she calls the Front-Line which is a greasy liquid she puts on the top of my head. That's what it feels like anyway. Beardy laughs his head off every time. "Come on Ollie," he says, "Come and get your Brylcreem." What is he on about?

Monday morning they both went out. Old Beardy had an appointment at the hospital to show a Consultant his funny walk. They were gone all morning. He got more than he bargained for. They did all sorts of tests. About time, I thought. I heard him on the telephone in the evening telling his Mum all about it. The trouble is, ever since Beardy has been home all this time with his problem, (the funny walk), he has been eating too much and not getting any exercise. Softy keeps telling him he mustn't go too far with a funny walk like that. While they were at the hospital, one of the 'tests' they did on Beardy was for his weight and now he's in trouble. Softy says he will have to stop putting his hand in the biscuit tin now he's 17 stone. Blimey! All the stick they give me about my 8 kilos and he's 17 stone. Now he's got to cut down. Then he might not walk so funny.

Tuesday was a good day. They were both out all day. I was still thinking it was a bit dodgy having them both off work though. I didn't like it the last time it happened. We didn't get along very well and by the end of the week I was locked up. Got out of the way. They said I was going to have a holiday. Some holiday! They shoved me in 'The Box' and took me to a place where there were about fifty chaps like me. All in for the same thing. All doing time. I was in for a week. So now you can see why I was jolly nervous about having them both at home again.

Wednesday lunchtime, just as I was having a nap on Beardy's bed, Softy came into the bedroom with Old Beardy close behind. "I'll make a fuss of Ollie while you get ready," she said. Look out, I thought. At least I lasted a week last time. Sure enough, there's Old Beardy behind me with 'The Box'. As soon as I spotted it, I was gone. Straight into the front room and under the small table. Big rumpus in the bedroom. Hee! Hee! Hee! Beardy was in trouble for being behind me with 'The Box' instead of in front. Into the front room came Softy who slowly lifted the table off me and grabbed me quick. Beardy was ready this time. The Box was open, door was up and I'm heading towards it. Just at the last minute, I got a second chance. As Softy was going to push me in, the door came down and hit her on the nose. She lost her grip and I was off. Straight into the back room and under an armchair. Beardy's fault again. In he came to get me. Each time he slowly moved the chair I slowly moved with it. All of a sudden, he laid the chair down flat and grabbed me, so I clung on to the carpet with all my might. No good though. He beat me this time and into 'The Box' I went.

Couldn't understand it. Off we went to see the man with the big needles. It wasn't a man this time though, it was a lady. I wonder if this is the Consultant for funny walks, I thought. Well, she checked me all over, said I was OK, but she would give me an injection anyway. What was that for? So I turned my back on her. Then it's Beardy's turn. Softy says, "I'm still worried about his weight." Must be talking about Beardy, he's the one with the weight problem. "Try giving him some light food," said the lady, "You can start with a bit of light biscuit and mix it in with his meat." Hee! Hee! Hee! I thought, that's got him, he usually has his biscuit with a cup of tea.

Bye for now,
Oliver.

Milton Keynes UK
Ingram Content Group UK Ltd.
UKHW020121071224
452277UK00001B/2

9 781917 293501